I dedicate this book to my three beautiful grandchildren Ruby, Eric and Walter, who are adventurous and love new challenges.

Opal Misses the Race

Fluttabee Tales

Book Three

Written by Ruth Jones

Illustrated by Patricia Goff

To Cal. With love Mandy & Hari (Ruth) Ruth Jones

Patricia Goff

This book belongs to

....

ISBN 978-1-7398048-2-4

Contents

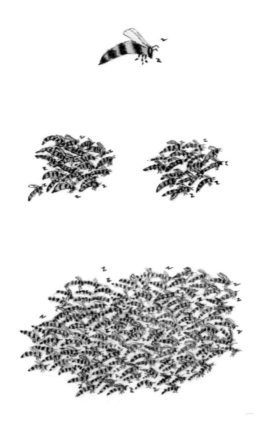

Have you ever watched the bees that live in your garden or in your local park?

Have you noticed that some fly around on their own and some fly around in groups. You may have been lucky enough to see a whole swarm of bees. A swarm can have thousands of bees in it, moving many bees from their hive to find another place to live.

Bees don't often go far from their own hives, choosing to take pollen from the flowers nearby. Occasionally though bees can fly further from their hives or collection area.

Perhaps today is one of those days.......

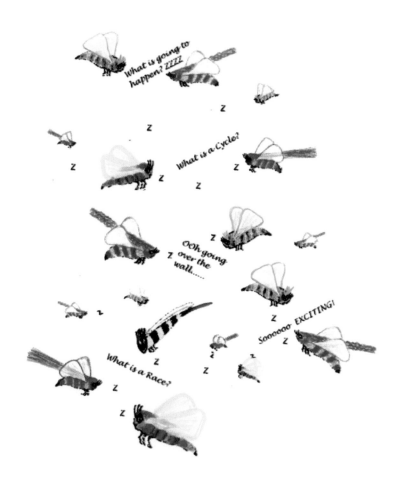

Chapter 1

Excitement in The Hive

There is lots of excitement in the valley of Fluttadale, hundreds of people are expected to arrive to watch the Cycle Race as it comes through the valley.

Opal, being a young Fluttabee, has no idea what to expect when she hears about the cycle race. She isn't even certain what a cycle race is…..
You see, her life in M's garden is gentle and quiet. The hive of Fluttabees don't see many people, just M, and her animals and the people who come to buy their honey.

Opal only knows that every Fluttabee in her hive has been buzzing about the race for weeks.
Yet nobody seems certain what is going to happen today…

Have you ever been to a cycle race? Do you know what happens at a big cycle race?

Fluttadale is part of the second day of three days of racing in Yorkshire. The valley is just a 2 kilometre stretch of the 120 kilometres ridden by the cyclists. Opal couldn't imagine flying for 1 kilometre never mind over a 100 kilometres. She's never been out of their garden. Her Queen Fluttabee, Diamond, does not allow it.

ONE HUNDRED
AND TWENTY
KILOMETRES!!!!!!!!!

z
z

It's early May and dawn is breaking over the valley. Opal and her friends Ruby, Sapphire, Emerald and Whiz are out collecting pollen from the garden flowers.

Opal and her friends normally have this time of day totally to themselves but they notice that people are already arriving in the valley.
Of course today is no ordinary day.
Today, is Race Day….

Queen Diamond has cancelled school for the day, saying it is more important to be part of the race day. To experience something new.

'Whiz, whoo, hurray, we're now free to play and explore' shouts Whiz, full of the excitement of what is to come.

School Closed
today
by order of
Queen Diamond

Chapter 2

Off to See The Race

Queen Diamond is allowing the young Fluttabees to leave the garden accompanied by their parents.
How exciting is that? Opal can hardly concentrate. 'What will we see, smell, feel, experience?' she asks herself.

Her imagination runs wild…. She has seen parts of the valley from the top of the Buddleia bush in the garden with Ruby. But to actually go over the wall, is both exciting and very scary.

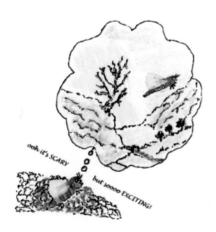

By late morning the Fluttabees are ready. Queen Diamond asks a small party to stay behind and keep the hive running, the rest of the families are free to fly out and enjoy the fun of the Big Race.

Emerald, Ruby, Sapphire, Opal and their parents meet in the Dining Hall. Whiz is also there as he lives with Emerald's family. Opal's Father offers to take Aqua and Topaz, as their parents are staying behind.

15 Fluttabees fly out across the garden, over the wall and towards the green hills in the distance.

Cows, sheep and goats graze in the fields below. People line the road and edges of the fields. Lots of two wheeled bikes lie on the grass, or against the walls. Their riders are dressed in the brightly coloured kit of their favourite cycling team. The noise is incredible as everyone chats, sings, laughs and shouts.

Suddenly above the Fluttabees, a very loud clattering, whirring sound is heard. The noise gets louder and louder. The air around throws them sideways, up and down, sending everyone into a spin and sucking them higher and higher into the air.

'What is going on?' scream the frightened Fluttabees.

Opal's father is head of the Air family, he quickly decides this is not a natural airflow.

'DIVE, DIVE' …. 'Fly down towards the ground, and stay low' he shouts.

As the group reach the calmer air lower down flying becomes easier. All are shaken by the experience. Opal's father reassures everyone it's fine, now he understands what just happened.

Being a magical Air Fluttabee, Opal's father creates a special bubble around their group to protect them from any other strange crafts they might meet.

Have you guessed what the strange craft could be?

This bright red helicopter carries the cameraman who is filming the crowds, and the route the cyclists will take. It will return later to film the actual race. It's a good job the Fluttabees now have the Air bubble around them for protection.

Opal, although scared by the helicopter experience, is still very excited. This is a whole new world out here today and she likes it. It makes her heart beat faster, her senses more alert, and her desire to have an adventure is greater than she can have ever imagined. She is always the cautious one, always questioning new things. Today is so, so different. Flying to the front of the group, she is keen to see everything. Looking for adventure.

As they fly above the road, watching the people in the crowd, Opal notices some people have climbed onto trees, walls, and even an old shepherds hut.

She guesses they have done this to get a better view of the race.

Time seems to go so quickly. No sooner than you can say 'Bob's your Uncle' - the pre race parade [called a 'Caravan' in racing] is entering the valley. The cars and lorries in the Caravan are decorated with the race sponsors' logos and products.

The Fluttabees stare in amazement.........

A 10 metre orange drinks bottle.
An enormous teddy bear throwing out sweets.
A lady on a huge swing singing.
What's that?
   A gigantic yellow and black bee with a man sitting on top. He's throwing out caps to the crowd. Boys, girls, men and women leap forward to catch them.
   This is crazy but exciting.

As the parade passes through, the crowds show off the gifts they have managed to catch. Clearly proud of what they have caught.

Opal looks on, 'if only I was big enough to catch one of the items.......' she whispers.

This is all so new and exciting for the Fluttabees. Can it get any better?

Opal's father takes away the Air bubble, feeling they are now safe from the helicopter.

'Brilliant' shouts Whiz.

What did you like best in the 'pre-race' Caravan Parade?

Chapter 3

What Are They?

As the Fluttabees fly further down the line of people, they come across a group dressed in yellow, with shiny black hats, large shiny black eyes, and black wings. What or who are they? Their bodies look human. But humans don't have wings and huge black eyes..... can you help the Fluttabees?

Can you explain what they are looking at?

Did you guess that they were humans, in fancy dress
BEE costumes?
Dressing up is part of the fun of Race day.
If you could dress up, what or who would you like to
be?

The crowd settle down again. Some people are
looking at the photos they've taken, others are showing
each other the gifts they caught in the pre-race Parade.
While others are taking more selfies, or having drinks
and snacks. Others are writing last minute messages
on the road with brightly coloured chalks.

Some are just quietly chatting or singing.

Some, are watching the small swarm of Fluttabees
as they fly by.....

As Opal and her group fly slowly past, more and more people start watching them.

Cries of 'What are they?'

'Have you ever seen anything like this before?'

'Does anyone know what these creatures are?' 'Look, there's green ones, and red ones, oh, look, blue ones, and white, blue and pink mottled ones.'

'Look how they sparkle, why are they different colours?'

'Can you see they have hair on their heads, their wings are butterfly shaped and flutter, but they still buzz?'

Do you remember 'M's Fluttabees are magical? Each Fluttabee belongs to one of life's natural elements - Earth [they are green Fluttabees], Fire [they are red Fluttabees], Water [they are bright blue Fluttabees], Air [they are soft marbled blue, pink, yellow and white Fluttabees]. Each family of Fluttabees have their own special powers linked to their element.

Imagine yourself in the crowd, watching and wondering. This small swarm of Fluttabees moving like a beautiful, colourful, sparkling, magical RAINBOW.

Chapter 4

The Race

Further down the dale the crowd started cheering and shouting. The first of the cyclists are coming. Suddenly, everyone around the Fluttabees stop looking at them. Now, they are jostling each other for the best view of the cyclists.

Cameras at the ready. Who will get the best pictures of the cyclists? Will they find their favourite riders?

Whoosh, Whoosh, Whoosh.. the lead riders rush by.

Seconds later, the next group are whizzing through. Gone in a flash.

The little group of Fluttabees stare in awe at the speed they go. Much faster than any Fluttabee can fly.

Look now, the Peloton is arriving. That's the name given to the main group of cyclists. A blur of colours pass. People shout, cheer, and clap. Some run alongside the riders. Cameras click.

Then they are gone.

The crowd turns to look for the next group.

'There, look, coming round the bend' someone shouts.

Again the crowd starts to cheer, shout and wave, to encourage the riders.

Some of the crowd push forward to get a better view.

The riders pass on through the cheering mass of people.

The Fluttabees buzz as loud as they can to cheer on the riders.

The next five minutes the crowd watch as individuals or small groups of cyclists pass by, all trying to catch up with the riders ahead.
Everybody stands looking, waiting and waiting.........
But no more riders arrive.

The race has passed by.

People start to pack up their belongings, say goodbye to new friends, find their way home.
Everyone is still excited by what they have seen today.

How do you think you would react in this crowd?
Would you be dressed in fancy dress?
Can you see yourself taking photos?
Cheering and shouting out names of the riders?
Running alongside the riders?
Sitting on your parent's shoulders?
Is the cycle race something that would excite you?

Meanwhile, while the crowd waited for the last cyclists, Opal's father signals it's time to return home. He quickly checks that all 15 Fluttabees are there. 9, 10, 11, 12, 13, 14………. he counts.

He counts again.

Still only 14, who is missing?

1 ……. 9 10 11 12 13 14 ??
who is missing??

Can you guess ?

Chapter 5

Where Can She Be?

It is Opal. Where can she be? Nobody had noticed her go.Everyone was too excited watching the race. The group is told to stay together, to look for Opal. They all search the field …… Nothing.

They fly
further down the
dale. Shouting
for her.

They search further up, then down the road………
Nothing.
They fly back over where they have been……
Nothing.
The people are leaving, the roadside is clearer………
Still nothing.
They search everywhere for her……. Nothing.

Their small group is starting to get very frightened.
Opal isn't the sort of Fluttabee to fly off on her own.
Something must have made her fly away.
Or has she had an accident?

What do you think might have happened to her?

It is while the group are making their second swoop
of the field and trees, near where they watched the
cyclists come through, that Emerald hears a distant
high pitched buzz.
It goes quiet, then he hears it again,
　　Buzz-z-z-z sss. sounding more frantic but very
distant and fuzzy. zzz-E-M-E-R-A-L-D-zzzz

'Has one of you just called my name?' he asks the
group.

'No' came their answer.

'It must be Opal then' he shouts, 'but where is she?'
'Quick fly low, spread out, look and listen, she has to be near, I can hear her.'

The few people that were still enjoying their afternoon in Fluttadale pay little attention to the small groups of Fluttabees slowly flying over the field, in and out of the trees.

One little boy watches with interest. He has been watching the Fluttabees for a while, wondering who they are, what they are doing. In fact he's been watching them since they arrived to watch the cycle race.

Sapphire listens intently, sure that she will hear Opal's call…. Nothing. It is Ruby who hears her this time, as she flies near the big oak tree.

'ZZZ- Help'
Calling the others, Ruby follows the sound. Flying round and round the tree, listening and searching.

Still no sign of Opal. Surely her beautiful sparkling white, pink and blue body and yellow wings would stand out against the dark colours of the tree and earth.

'Zzzz-help-zzz -me...
Ruby and Emerald stop.
'It's Opal' they both shout.
They look. Still nothing, only the tree.

'What's that hanging from the branch?' cries Sapphire.
A small brown bag.
Can the sound be coming from there?
Is Opal inside this bag?

Emerald, Ruby and Sapphire rush to investigate.

Opal's father urges caution, and quickly flies down to take control.

'Opal are you inside?' gently asks Opal's father.

'Zzzyezzz it's ssss meee, father' whispers Opal.

'Are you hurt?' Opal's mother asks.

'Zz-just bruised and scared-zzz' Opal cries.

'Try not to move. We will think what to do. You'll be safe soon' says Opal's father.

The fathers meet to plan a rescue.

Emerald, Ruby, Sapphire, Topaz and Whiz huddle together to discuss what they might do.

What do you think you would do?

Their mothers and Aqua say encouraging words to Opal to help her feel better and less afraid.

Whoosh …. What was that??

'zz help.' 'What'zzz happening??' 'Where are we zzzz?'
Came the muffled shouts and buzzing.

'Where have the children gone?' screams Ruby's
mother

The small boy is
standing
near the tree, holding
a large green net on
the end of a long
stick. On the floor
next to him is a small
basket with the lid
open.

He looks excited and
happy.

Carefully he holds one side of the green net, and places
the net over the open basket.

The net is making a lot of angry buzzing noises.

He shakes the net and quickly closes the lid to the basket. The noises stop. Seconds later they restart, only this time sounding more muffled.

The little boy smiles, he has caught the young Fluttabees in his green net, and put them into his basket.

Can you imagine how you would feel if this happened to you.......

Five confused and frightened Fluttabees in the dark.

What will happen to them now?..........

It is Whiz who takes charge inside the basket. He tells everyone to stay calm, to breathe slowly, and think of pleasant things. As he talks, the group slowly feel calmer. They adjust as soft rays of light work their way through the woven walls of straw and give an eerie light in the basket. Air drifts in through the gaps in the weave, which is good.

Whiz checks each one of them for injuries. Luckily they are just shaken and a little bruised.

Whiz and Emerald push the lid, but it does not move. There is no way out.

'At least we can see each other and breathe fresh air' says Sapphire.

Outside their fathers fly to the basket, and are happy their young ones are all ok.

Now there are two sets of Fluttabees, in two separate prisons.

An adventure has turned into a dangerous situation.

Not a good ending to a wonderful day.

The young boy looks pleased with himself. He now has 6 of the most wonderful creatures he has ever seen to show his friends at school.

He stands watching the other Fluttabees flying around his bag and basket, never guessing that they are the parents and guardians of his captives.

Thankfully he has enough Fluttabees to show his friends. He makes no attempt to catch the others.

And what a prize he has. This is going to make him the talk of school. He knows everyone will want to see his beautiful creatures.

'I must find a jam jar I can put them in, so they don't fly away while I'm showing them' thinks the boy.

Opal's father knows he has to do something quickly, before the boy's family start to pack up and leave.

How can they use all their special powers to help the young Fluttabees?

Flying around the bag hanging on the low branch, then to the basket resting between the same tree's roots, an idea starts to form.

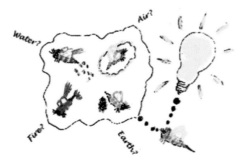

He talks to the Fluttabees.
They decide what to do.

Emerald's father and mother stay at the tree.

Sapphire's mother and Ruby's father fly to a nearby bush that is close to the boy's family car.

The remaining Fluttabees gather near the tree to help Opal's family.

Opal's mother explains to the young friends how the other Fluttabees are going to try to set them free.

Chapter 6

Will Their Plan Work?

Suddenly the air feels colder, the breeze swirls around the tree, it swirls around the boy's picnic table knocking cups and plates to the floor.

The breeze grows stronger and whips around the boy's legs, making him trip over.

The stronger breeze shakes the branches.

Groans and creaks escape from the tree as it's roots move, knocking the basket gently to one side.

Whoosh, a sudden burst of
fire erupts from the bush
near the boy's car.
Ruby's father watches to
make sure his fire burns
safely. Sapphire's mother is
there too.

The distraction is working..........

The trees branches bend in the
now strong swirling wind. The
branch with the bag, bends so
far down, its branches touch the
ground. The bag gently rolls
onto the soft moss around the
roots. Ruby's mother flashes a
tiny flame, to burn through the
string at the top of the bag.

Aqua is watching the bag
carefully, as soon as the string
is broken and before it burns
the bag, she squirts water
onto the flames to put the fire
out.

Together Aqua and Ruby's
mother can now pull the bag
open.

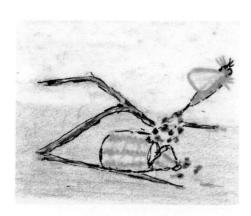

Emerald's mother is
there at the basket,
using her powers to
guide the tree root to
open the lid.

The young Fluttabees escape from their prisons.
Hooray……..

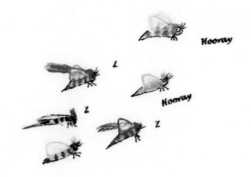

They are safe.
But there is still work to do.

The boy and his family wildly run to pick up the picnic things and try to put out the fire.

Ruby's father and Sapphire's mother are watching the bush carefully. The fire is safely burning.

Now is the time for Sapphire's mother to put out the fire. By making water from a nearby stream spray over the burning bush, the fire is out within seconds and the bush steams.

Do you think anyone noticed a group of Fluttabees using their magic to make the wind blow, the fires burn, the trees and earth move and the water flow?

As soon as the rescue is over, the Fluttabees go back to repair any damage to the bush, tree and stream.

Looking after nature is very important to them.

The boy's family will never understand. They only know they will not come to Fluttadale again. Too many scary unexplained things happen here.

The boy still has an interesting story to tell his friends at school. Thankfully, he has no Fluttabees to show.

But will they believe him?

The young Fluttabees are safe and sound. Happy to be back with their families. They will have their own stories to tell.

Opal says she might not be so adventurous next time, flying off on her own brought all this trouble onto the Fluttabees.

Oh dear I MIGHT NOT be quite so adventurous next time......

The Fluttabees didn't stay to watch the boy and his family gather the rest of their scattered belongings. They didn't want anyone to end up in the basket or bag ever again.

After quick checks, and many hugs, they all fly high into the now quiet sky. They follow Opal's father as he leads them home to 'M's cottage. He creates a large bubble around the long trail of Fluttabees to keep them safe and together. The group have never looked so pleased and happy and relieved to be back inside the walls of their beautiful garden.

Who do you think tells their story first?

The Fluttabees prove that working as a team, using everyone's strengths is the best way to solve a problem or situation. Those same strengths are always used to repair any damage they might have caused.

Even if you're on your own, think about your strengths and what you can do safely to help someone.

Opal's Wish

Enjoy life, be adventurous, but be cautious too. Think first, am I safe? Do friends and family know where I am? Is my action going to affect someone else?

If you do get into trouble, or you see someone who needs help, try to stay calm, breathe slowly and think about your situation before you react.

If you can get help, do so - shout, phone, wave, make any sort of noise to get someone's attention.

Have fun and learn from watching tiny creatures. Remember if you pick a creature up to study it, please put it back straight afterwards.

Best wishes from Opal.

The Fluttabee Challenge

1. Find out what causes a swarm of bees to leave their hive.

2. Which type of bee flies in a swarm, and which type of bees fly on their own?

3. Discuss with family and friends what you need to do to keep yourself safe when you are outside playing.

4. Find out the names of the famous cycle races that have taken place in Britain in the last 10 years.

5. Find out the names of 5 famous British long distance cyclists and learn about their lives.

6. Draw the fancy dress you would like to wear at a cycle race.

Thank you for reading
'Opal Misses the Race'

We hope you enjoyed our book.
Have fun watching the bees near
you.

We would love to hear from you.
Perhaps send us a drawing of a bee
you have seen.
You can reach us on
fluttabeetales@hotmail.com

Watch out for Book 4
'Emerald Saves the Day'

Best Wishes
Ruth and Patricia

Printed in Great Britain
by Amazon

77424904R00027